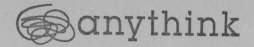anythink

GOODNIGHT MERMAID

WRITTEN BY K. J. OCEANAK | ILLUSTRATED BY ALLIE OGG

Manufactured by: Friesens Corporation • Altona, Canada • July 2020 • Job #266655 • Printed in Canada

Published by: Bailiwick Press • 309 East Mulberry Street, Fort Collins, Colorado 80524 • www.bailiwickpress.com • ISBN 978-1-934649-80-0

25 24 23 22 21 20   10 9 8 7 6 5 4 3 2 1

BAILIWICK PRESS

In the deep blue sea,
there were fishes with sails,
crustaceans and whales,
and a marvel of...

...mermaids with magnificent tails.

And there were three little selkies sitting on whelkies.

And nautical nymphs playing polo with shrimps.

And submarine tunes.

And a waterworld moon.

And synchronized swirls. And pearls upon pearls.

And plunges and leaps. And pledges to keep.

And Her Majesty the Merqueen reigning over the deep.

Goodnight discovery. Goodnight schools.

Goodnight bright and brimming pools.

Goodnight bounty. Goodnight hearts.
Goodnight oceanic arts.

Goodnight mermaids.
Goodnight tails.

Goodnight waves and whopping whales.

Goodnight pearls. Goodnight swirls. Goodnight tunes and goodnight moon.

Goodnight selkies. Goodnight whelkies. Goodnight nymphs and goodnight shrimps.

Goodnight shimmer and aquamarine.
Goodnight wise and benevolent queen.

Goodnight courage. Goodnight power.
Goodnight grit in this late, late hour.

Goodnight friends with tails unfurled.

Goodnight blue wonder that gives life to our world.

MERMAIDOLOGY

Mermaids are half human, half marine mammal. They can breathe both under and above the water.

Selkies are cousins to mermaids. They're part human, part seal. Water nymphs are tiny fairies who live underwater.

Mermaids have fluked tails like whales, but mermaids' tails sometimes change color when their moods change.

Each mermaid is granted the privilege of transformation once a year. Her tail transfigures into legs, and for one week she walks among us.

The Merqueen carries a trident and has been alive for thousands of years.

Mermaids are known for their creativity. They're musicians, artists, designers, builders, and scientists.

Mermaids eat kelp and sea grasses. When they sneak onto tropical islands and ships, they enjoy tasting human food and adore lemon-meringue pie.

Mermaids take care of our miraculous oceans, but they need our help.

THE MERMAID'S PLEDGE

Before earning their mermaid tiaras,
all mermaids-in-training learn this pledge by heart.
Place both hands over your merheart and repeat aloud.

I am a mermaid, lively and free.
I swim with my friends in the saltwater sea.

I love every fathom and reef that we roam.
I pledge to protect and help care for our home.

Each creature is crucial, the big and the small.
I pledge to be kind and respectful to all.

The ocean's my oyster, from island to shore.
I pledge to stay curious, learn, and explore.

I'm wildly creative. I rock boats by choice.
I pledge to make waves and to sing with my voice.

I'm fierce and I'm bold, hardworking and strong.
I pledge to plunge headfirst when chance comes along.

I'm flukily me, and you're flukily you.
We pledge to be dreamers, for merdreams come true.